Emma Lundy
29.1.85

The Oxford Music Picture Word Book

Sarah Williams

Oxford
Oxford University Press
New York Melbourne
1984

Oxford music books for children
The Oxford First Companion to Music by
                Kenneth and Valerie McLeish
The Oxford Junior Companion to Music by Michael Hurd
Heroes and Heroines in Music by Wendy-Ann Ensor
More Heroes and Heroines in Music by Wendy-Ann Ensor
   (plus cassette covering both books)
At Home with Music by Jean Gilbert

Oxford University Press, Walton Street, Oxford OX2 6DP

London New York Toronto
Delhi Bombay Calcutta Madras Karachi
Kuala Lumpur Singapore Hong Kong Tokyo
Nairobi Dar es Salaam Cape Town
Melbourne Auckland

and associated companies in
Beirut Berlin Ibadan Mexico City Nicosia

Oxford is a trade mark of Oxford University Press

First published 1984

British Library Cataloguing in Publication Data
Williams, Sarah
The Oxford music picture word book
1. Music—Dictionaries, Juvenile
I Title
780'.3'21   ML100

ISBN 0 19 311329 5

Designed by Ann Samuel
Illustrated by Joanna Stubbs

Printed in Hong Kong

Acknowledgements
We are grateful to the following for permission to
reproduce their copyright material:

Photographs
p. 28–29 Armstrong, Chung, Fletcher, Grapelli,
Yama'Shita The Decca Record Co Ltd; Beatles Rex
Features; Blades C Pryke; Bream Sophie Baker;
Callas Houston Rogers; Fonteyn BBC Hulton Picture
Library; Galway RCA/London Artists; Goossens C A
Busby; Guy Jim Four; Holliger Ingpen and Williams Ltd;
Kanawa CBS; Lill, Menuhin Harold Holt Ltd; Munrow
Reg Wilson; Nureyev S A Gorlinsky Ltd; Previn
Harrison/Parrott Ltd; Primrose Nigel Hunt; Segovia,
Tortelier Ibbs and Tillett Ltd; Simon and Garfunkel Griffin
Records; Wick Don Williams; Williams Sophie Baker.

Music and text
p. 47 'Yellow Submarine' by John Lennon and Paul
McCartney (ATV Music Limited)©1966 Northern Songs
Limited. All rights for the U.S.A., Mexico and the Philippines
controlled by Maclen Music, Inc. Used by permission. All
rights reserved; p. 47 'Morning has broken', words by
Eleanor Farjeon from *The Childrens' Bells* (OUP)

Contents

Part 1 A music dictionary a–z 5–27
A gallery of performers past and present 28

Part 2 Musical topics
The orchestra 30
Instrumental families 32
Groups and bands 36
Written music 38
Rhythm 39
How many beats? 39
Inside a recording studio 40
Different types of music 41
Music from around the world 42
Composers and the countries they come from 44
Different songs 46
Opposites 48
Dances from around the world 50
Voices 52
Different dances 52
Festivals and musical occasions 53

Part 3 Sound and action words 57–58

Part 4 Sound pictures 59–64
The four seasons 61
A witch's cavern 62
A walk in the rain 62
Under water 63
A farmyard 63
The seaside 64
Journey into space 64

To parents and teachers

The Music Picture Word Book has four main sections.

The dictionary

There are 243 words in this section in alphabetical order. They are selected as being the words that younger children are most likely to come into contact with whether in their listening, reading, in the classroom or in the wider area of general experience. Each word is illustrated with a picture and a simple definition or contextual phrase. The alphabet is printed at the top of each page with the letter on the page highlighted, to enable the child to see at a glance if he or she must turn forewards or backwards to find a particular word. The final pages in this section present a gallery of performers past and present. Some names are legendary, for example Maria Callas, others have been or are still influential contributors in their own musical specialities. I hope each aspiring young musician will find at least one new face here with a name they can listen out for in the future.

Musical topics

These pages include labelled drawings of instrumental families; a recording studio; written music; musical 'opposites', together with world maps to illustrate information about different countries of the world and their influences on music, song and dance. There is a collection of composers and the countries they come from for children to see at a glance which areas of the world are most influential in their musical heritage. It is my intention that these pages will stimulate general observations and discussions and provide the basis for simple topic work. The final pages in this section refer children to 12 festivals or occasions in which music, singing or dancing are performed.

Sound and action words

These pages include 'loud' and 'soft' words, ways of 'playing' words, ways of 'saying' words, and ways of 'moving' words, collections of words for children to explore and enjoy whether just saying them, playing them or moving to them.

Sound pictures

These pages are intended as a starting point for children to improvise and make up their own music. They contain seven pictures labelled with suggestions as to the type of musical illustrations the children can investigate and explore.

a

accompaniment

the guitar playing the accompaniment

accordion

squeezing an accordion

Albert Hall

a large concert hall in London

allegro

an Italian word meaning fast and lively

alp horn

a wind instrument from Switzerland

audience

people listening to a concert

b

background music

music in the supermarket

bagpipes

a piper playing the bagpipes

balalaika

a Russian folk instrument

ballet

a dance that tells a story

5

bamboo pipe

blowing a bamboo pipe

band

a Salvation Army band

bandstand

the bandstand in the park

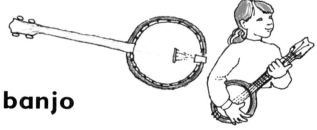

banjo

an American folk instrument

bassoon

a low-sounding woodwind instrument

bass drum

a large low-sounding drum

bass recorder

the lowest sounding recorder

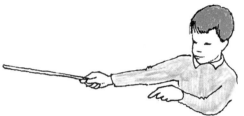

baton

the stick a conductor uses

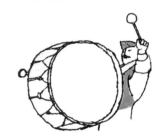

beat (n)

the beat of the bass drum

beat(v)

the conductor beats time for the band

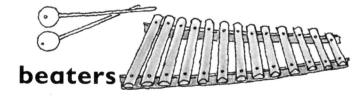

beaters

beaters for a xylophone

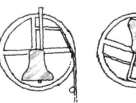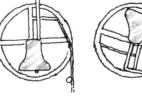

bell

the bells in a church steeple

Blues

a sad jazz song

bongos

a pair of small drums
played by hand

bouzouki

a Greek folk instrument

bow

a bow for a string instrument

brass

the trumpet, horn, trombone and
tuba are brass instruments

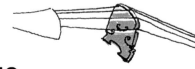

bridge

the bridge of a violin

bugle

a brass instrument

busker

a street musician

calypso

a folk song from the West Indies

carnival

a festival with singing
and dancing

Carnival of the animals

a piece of music by Saint-Saëns

a b **c** d e f g h i j k l m n o p q r s t u v w x y z

carol

a song we sing at Christmas time

cassette

a tape to play on
the cassette recorder

castanets

Spanish dancing with castanets

celesta

an instrument which makes
a tinkling sound

cello

a low-sounding wooden
string instrument

chime bars

metal bars that sound like a bell

choir

a group of singers in church

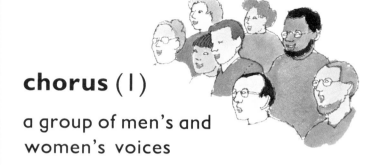

chorus (1)

a group of men's and
women's voices

Nowell Nowell
Nowell Nowell
Born is the King
of Israel

chorus (2)

singing the chorus after each verse

clarinet

a woodwind instrument
with a single reed

classical

the kind of music composed by
Haydn and Mozart

claves

two wooden sticks

composer

someone who makes up music

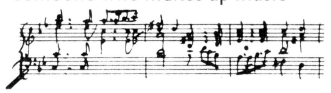

composition

music made up by a composer

concert

a musical entertainment

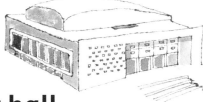

concert hall

a place where concerts are heard

concertina

an instrument you squeeze

concerto

a piece of music for
soloist and orchestra

conducting

showing the beat and
feel of the music

conductor

the person who conducts
the orchestra

Coppélia

a famous ballet about a doll

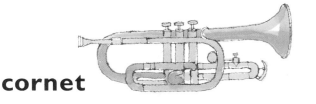

cor anglais

a woodwind instrument
that sounds like an oboe

cornet

an instrument in a brass band

cymbal

clashing the cymbals

country and western

American folk music

Covent Garden

an opera house in London

d

dance (v)

to move to music

descant

a tune above the main tune

disc

a record

disc jockey

a disc jockey putting on a record

discothèque/disco

dancing at the disco

double bass

the largest, lowest-sounding string instrument

drum

beating a drum

drum kit

a set of drums

duet

music for two players

e

early music

music of the Middle Ages

electric guitar

plugging in an electric guitar

ensemble

musicians playing together

euphonium

one of the largest
instruments in a brass band

f

fanfare

a trumpet fanfare
for a special occasion

festival

Carnival is a West Indian festival

fiddle

a violin used in folk music

fife

a soldier with musket,
fife and drum

film music

music played as
background for a film

flute

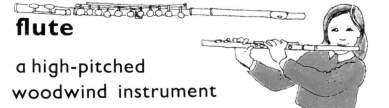

a high-pitched
woodwind instrument

folk song

a song everyone knows

forte

an Italian word meaning loud

French horn

a brass instrument

g

gig

a slang word for a concert

glockenspiel

sounds like tiny bells

gong

banging a gong

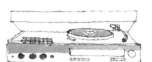

gramophone

a record player

grand piano

a large keyboard instrument

group

a pop group

guitar

strumming the guitar

h

a b c d e f g **h** **i** j k l m n o p q r s t u v w x y z

hand bells

ringing hand bells

Hansel and Gretel

a famous fairy tale opera

harmonium

playing a harmonium in church

harp

a Welsh girl plucking her harp

harpsichord

a keyboard instrument which sounds soft and gentle

hunting horn

a huntsman's horn

hurdy gurdy

turning a hurdy gurdy, a medieval instrument

hymn

a Christian song of worship

i

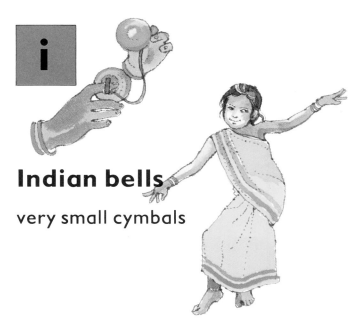

Indian bells

very small cymbals

Indian dancers

Indian dancers use their arms and bodies as they dance

instruments

some musicians with their instruments

j

jam session

jazz musicians playing together for fun

jazz

a type of music started by black people in America

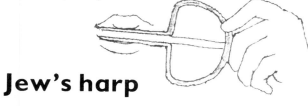

Jew's harp

twanging a jew's harp in your mouth

milk has gotta lotta bottle

jingle

a tune used for an advertisement

jingles

small bells

juke box

choose your favourite record to play on the juke box

k

kazoo

blowing the kazoo makes a buzzing sound

kettle drum

a large brass or copper drum that can be tuned

key

pressing down the key gives you the note

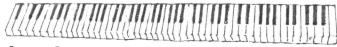

keyboard

the piano keyboard

l

La Scala, Milan

a famous opera house in Italy

leader

the first violin is the leader of the orchestra

legato

an Italian word for a smooth sound

lullaby

a rocking song for a baby

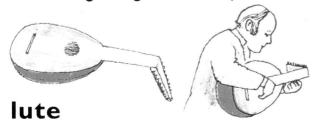

lute

a medieval stringed instrument

lyre

a very old string instrument

m

madrigal

a song sung in parts

Magic Flute

a famous opera by Mozart

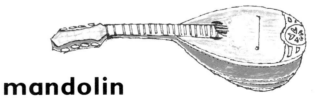

mandolin

an Italian string instrument

maracas

dried seeds rattle inside maracas

medieval music

music written before the year 1500

megaphone

helps your voice to be heard from far away

melodica

a keyboard instrument that is blown

melody

a tune

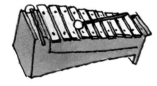

metallophone

a percussion instrument made of metal

metronome

helps to fix the speed of a piece of music

Metropolitan Opera House

an opera house in New York

microphone

makes the sound louder

military band

a brass band for soldiers

minstrel

a musician who travelled from town to town performing music for money

morris dance

a lively English folk dance

mouth organ

an instrument often played by folk and street musicians

musical

a play with music

music hall

a place where variety shows are held

music stand

holds the music for the performer

mute

a mute for an instrument quietens the sound

National Anthem

a country's special song

note

describes a sound

nursery rhyme

Baa Baa Black Sheep is a nursery rhyme

Nutcracker

a famous ballet by Tchaikovsky

oboe

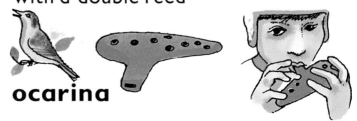

a woodwind instrument with a double reed

ocarina

a South American instrument that sounds like a bird

octave

eight notes up or down the scale

opera

a play with singing instead of speaking

opera house

a place where operas are performed

orchestra

instruments playing together

organ

a keyboard instrument found in churches

organist

the person who plays the organ

overture

music played at the beginning of the performance

p

panpipes

blowing some panpipes

pantomime

a play at Christmas time with singing and dancing

pause

a sign which means wait

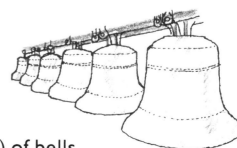

peal

a peal (set) of bells

pedal

this piano has two pedals

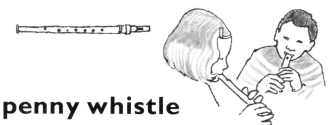

penny whistle

a metal folk instrument you blow

percussion

any instrument you strike or hit

performer

someone playing to an audience

piano (1)

an Italian word meaning soft

piano (2)

a keyboard instrument

piano tuner

a person who tunes and repairs pianos

piccolo

the highest-sounding woodwind instrument

pit

the place where the orchestra sits in an opera house

pitch

a flute has a high pitch sound a double bass has a low pitch sound

pizzicato

plucking a string instrument

plectrum

a plastic disc to pluck a guitar

polka

a lively dance

pop

popular music

Proms

a musical event in London

programme

details of a concert

pungi

a snake charmer's instrument

q

quartet

four musicians playing together

quintet

five musicians playing together

r

raga

an Indian melody

ragtime

a kind of jazz

rattle

different rattles to shake

recital

a soloist giving a recital

record (n)

an LP – a long playing record

record (v)

to record music from the radio

record player

listening to records
on the record player

recorder

a woodwind instrument you play
in school

recording studio

a place where records are made

reed

oboe, clarinet saxophone, bassoon
these instruments are played by
blowing through a reed of dried
grass or cane

reggae

a kind of Jamaican music

rehearsal

practice before a concert

rests

signs which mean silence

rhyme

words which sound alike

rhythm

tick tock, tick tock is
the rhythm of this clock

rock

a type of music

round

London's burning is a round

S

Saint Cecilia

the patron saint of music

saxophone

a wind instrument used in a jazz band

scale

a set of notes in order

score

each performer's part is written down in the score

Scottish dancers

dancers from Scotland

scraper

playing a scraper

sea shanty

a sailor's song

side drum

a drum that makes a rattling sound

sitar

an Indian string instrument

slide

helps the trombone
play more notes

snare drum

same as side drum

soloist

a violin soloist with an orchestra

spiritual

a religious song from America

staccato

an Italian word for a short sound

stave

notes are written on five lines
called a stave

steel drums

 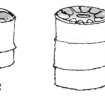

tuned instruments made
from old oil drums

street cries

sung by street traders to advertise
their wares

string

putting new strings on a guitar

Swan Lake

a famous ballet by Tchaikovsky

symphony

many instruments
sounding together

synthesizer

an electronic instrument

tabla

two Indian drums played with hands and fingers

tambour

a tambourine without bells

tambourine

a folk instrument to shake or tap

tambura

an Indian lute

tap dancers

special shoes make the tapping sound

tape

a reel of tape for the tape recorder

tenor recorder

one of the lowest-sounding recorders

timpani

another name for kettle drums

tom tom

small drums

treble recorder

a low-sounding recorder

triangle

a metal percussion instrument

trio

three musicians playing together

trombone
slide

a brass instrument with a slide

trumpet
valve

a brass instrument
with three valves

tuba

the lowest-sounding
brass instrument

tubular bells
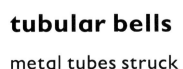

metal tubes struck
with drum sticks

tune
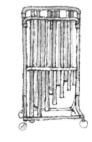

playing an accompaniment
to the tune

tuning fork

helps us to get the right note

tutu

a ballet dancer's dress

u

ukelele

a type of small guitar

upright piano

a piano at home and school

v

valve

a trumpet has three valves

variety show

entertainment with singing and dancing

vibraphone

an electronic instrument used in jazz

Vienna Boys' Choir

a famous choir from Austria

vocal cords

part of your voice

viola

a string instrument a little larger and lower-sounding than a violin

violin

the highest-sounding instrument in the violin family

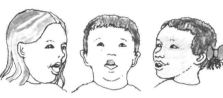

voice

your instrument with which you can sing and speak

W

waltz

a dance

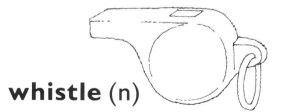

whistle (n)

a football referee uses a whistle

whistle (v)

to blow through your lips

wind band

our school wind band

wood block

a Chinese wood block

woodwind

flute, clarinet, oboe, bassoon
wind instruments originally made
from wood

x

xylophone

a wooden percussion instrument

y

yell

shouting at the top of your voice

yodelling

a sound sung high
and low very quickly

z

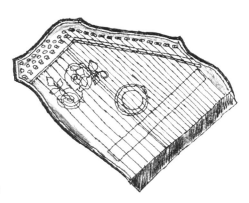

zither

a stringed folk instrument

A gallery of performers past and present

Louis Armstrong was an American jazz trumpeter

André Previn is a famous conductor

Ravi Shankar is a sitar player

The Beatles were a British pop group of the 1960s

Andrés Segovia is a famous Spanish guitarist

Stefan Grapelli is a jazz violinist

Maria Callas was a famous opera singer

James Galway is a flute player

Simon and Garfunkel are American singers

Kyung Wha Chung is a violinist from Korea

David Munrow was a player of early instruments

Stomu Yama'Shita is a Japanese drummer

Margot Fonteyn is a famous ballet dancer

John Lill is a pianist

Paul Tortelier is a cello player

Rudolph Nureyev is a famous ballet dancer

Denis Wick is a trombone player

Sidonie Goossens is a harpist

John Williams is a guitarist

Kiri Te Kanawa is a singer from New Zealand

Barry Tuckwell is a horn player

Yehudi Menuhin is a violinist

John Fletcher is a tuba player

Placido Domingo is an Italian opera singer

James Blades is a percussionist

Heinz Holliger is an oboe player

Julian Bream is a guitar and lute player

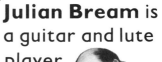
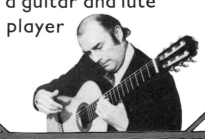

Barry Guy is a double bass player

Benny Goodman is a jazz clarinettist

William Primrose was a viola player

The orchestra

triangle

tubular bells

glockenspiel

harpist

horns

flutes

piccolo

2nd violins

1st violins

music stands

microphones

leader of orchestra

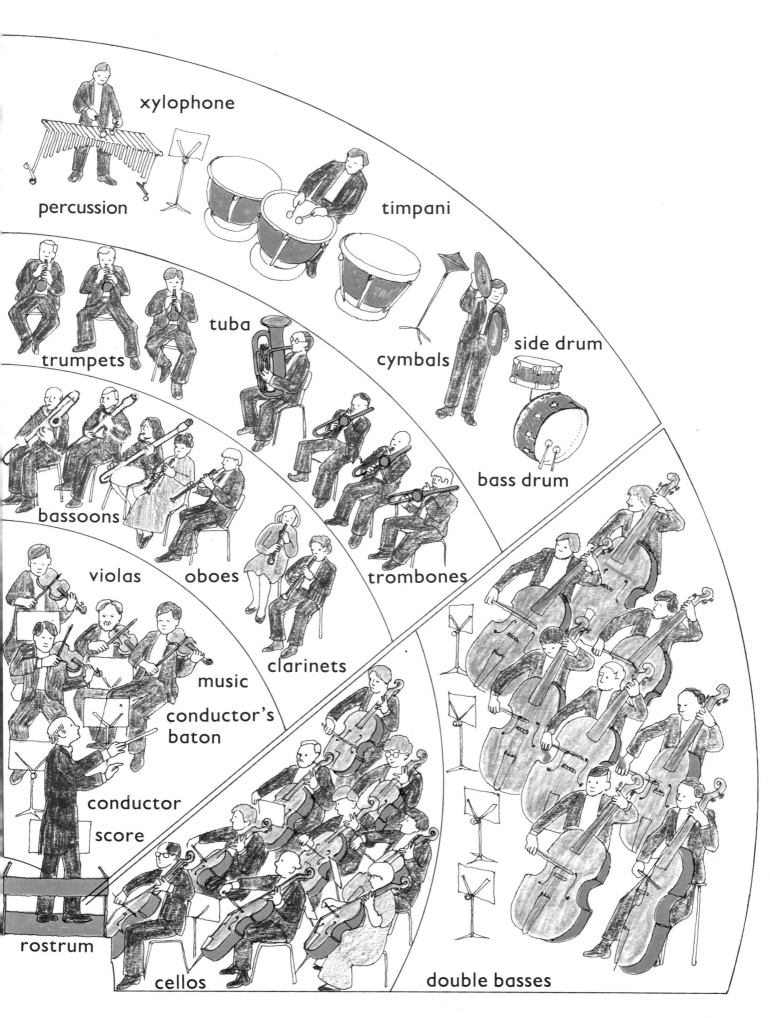

xylophone

percussion

timpani

trumpets

tuba

cymbals

side drum

bassoons

bass drum

violas

oboes

trombones

music

conductor's
baton

clarinets

conductor

score

rostrum

cellos

double basses

31

Instrumental families

Violin family

violin

double bass

cello

viola

Woodwind family

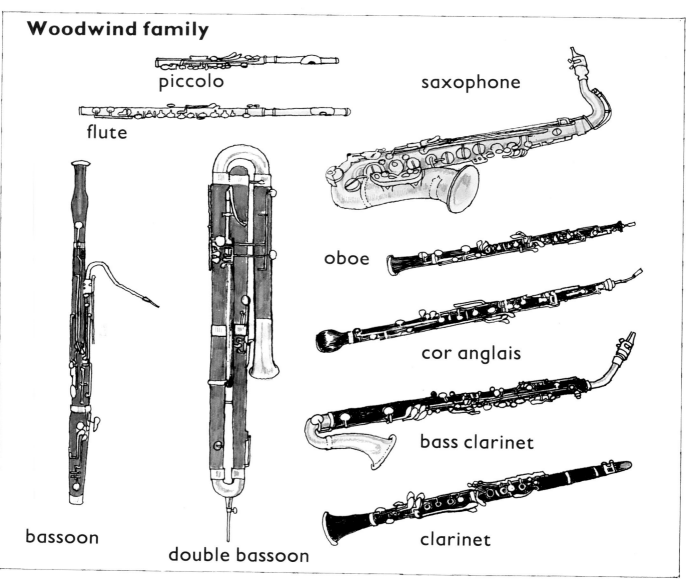

piccolo

saxophone

flute

oboe

cor anglais

bass clarinet

bassoon

clarinet

double bassoon

Brass family

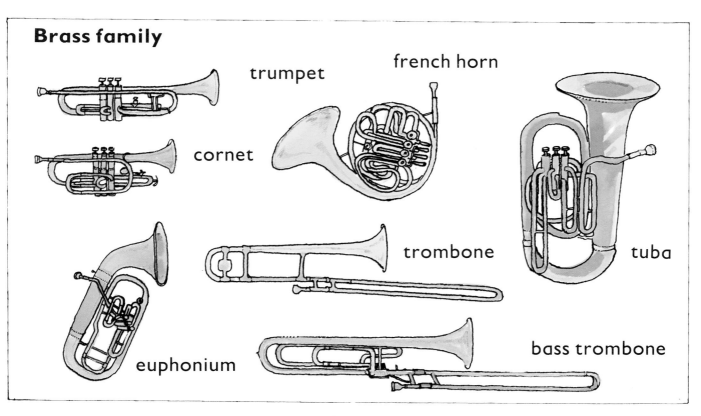

trumpet

french horn

cornet

trombone

tuba

euphonium

bass trombone

Keyboard family

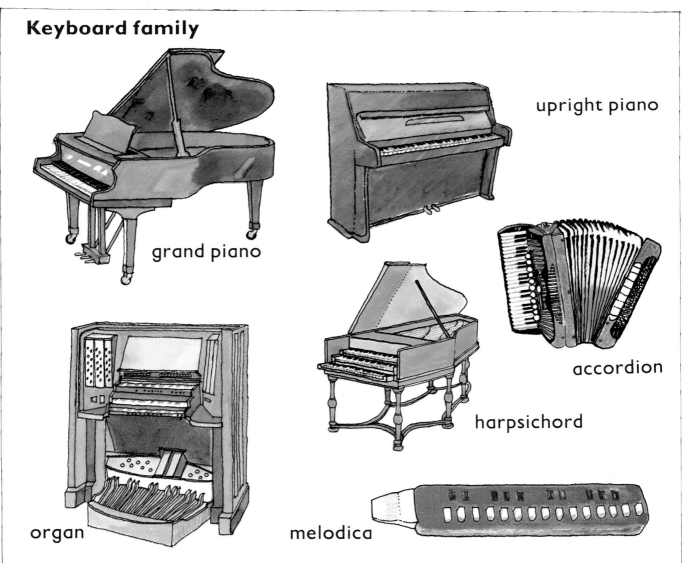

upright piano

grand piano

accordion

harpsichord

organ

melodica

Percussion family

Indian bells

sleigh bells

castanets

claves

woodblock

guiro

maracas

tambourine

tambour

triangle

cymbal

tubular bells

celesta

xylophone

glockenspiel

metallophone

tom tom

side drum

timpani

congos

bass drum

bongos

Recorder consort (family)

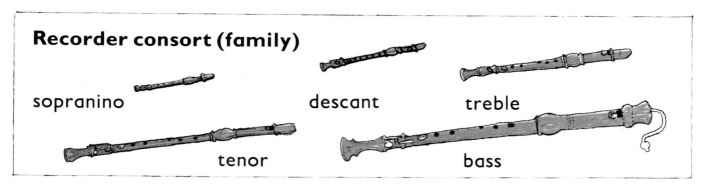

sopranino

descant

treble

tenor

bass

Drum family

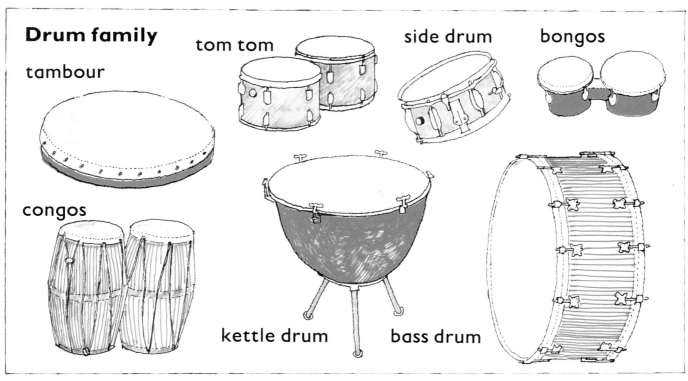

tambour

tom tom

side drum

bongos

congos

kettle drum

bass drum

Guitar family

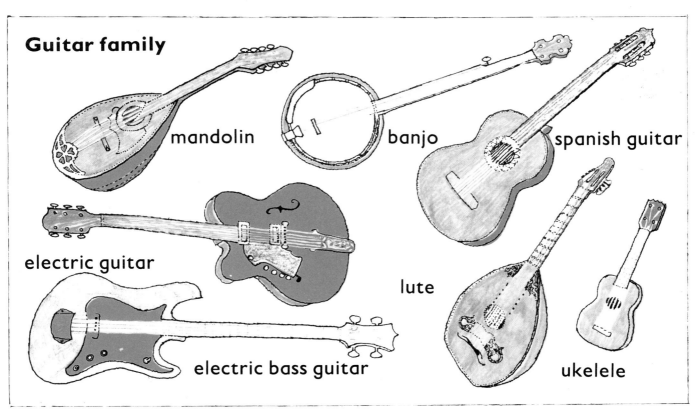

mandolin

banjo

spanish guitar

electric guitar

lute

electric bass guitar

ukelele

Groups and bands

Brass band

Wind band

Jazz band

Rock band

Steel band

Reggae band

Dance band

Orchestra

Instruments of a pop group

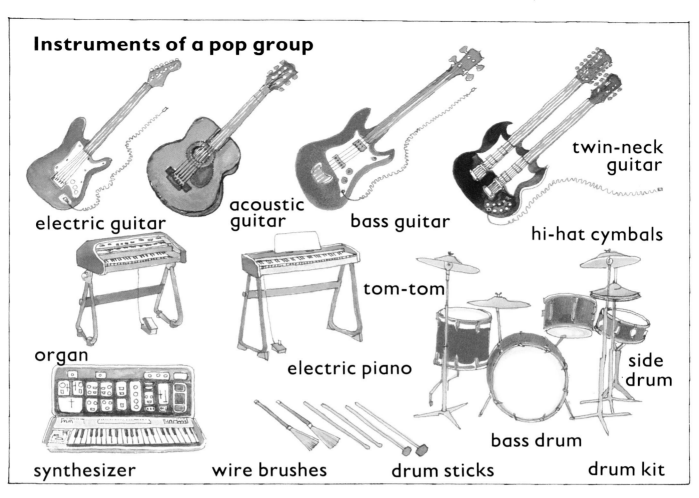

electric guitar

acoustic guitar

bass guitar

twin-neck guitar

hi-hat cymbals

organ

tom-tom

electric piano

side drum

synthesizer

wire brushes

drum sticks

bass drum

drum kit

Instruments of a brass band

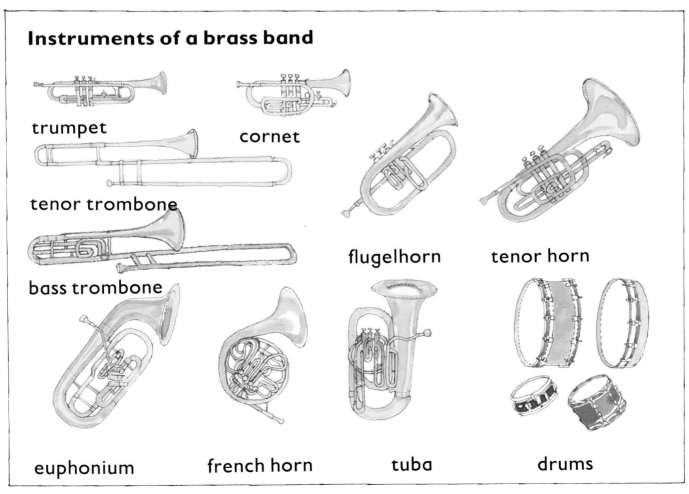

trumpet

cornet

tenor trombone

flugelhorn

tenor horn

bass trombone

euphonium

french horn

tuba

drums

37

Written music

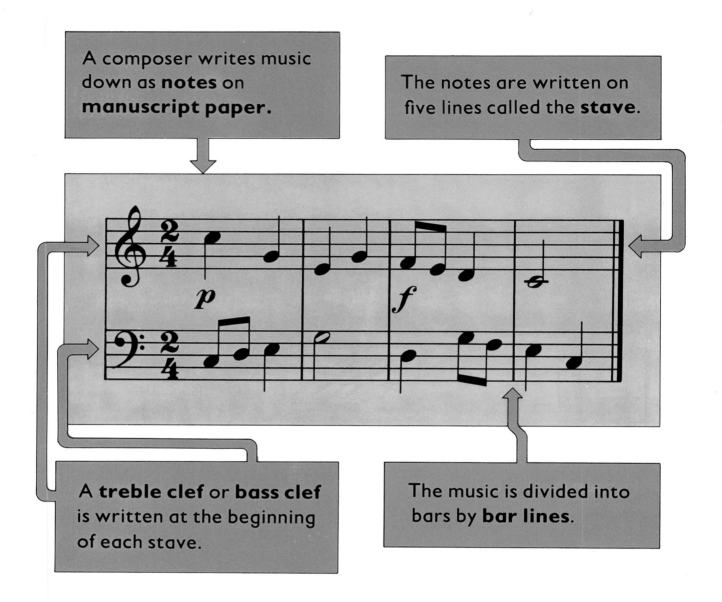

A composer writes music down as **notes** on **manuscript paper.**

The notes are written on five lines called the **stave**.

A **treble clef** or **bass clef** is written at the beginning of each stave.

The music is divided into bars by **bar lines**.

A composer writes a sign to show whether the music is to sound loud or quiet.

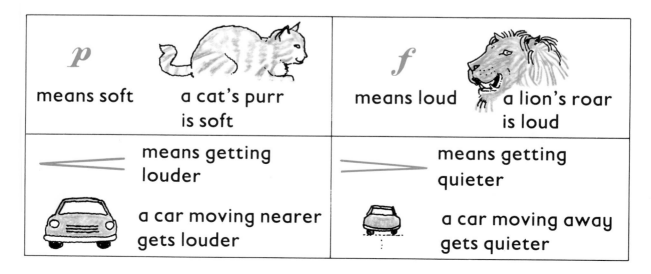

p		*f*	
means soft	a cat's purr is soft	means loud	a lion's roar is loud
∕	means getting louder	∕	means getting quieter
	a car moving nearer gets louder		a car moving away gets quieter

Rhythm

A rhythm is a pattern in music. It is the **beat** or **pulse** of the sound.
A rhythm is written down in notes.

Baa, baa, black sheep,   have you   a—ny wool?

Each note (a **crotchet**) equals one beat.
The numbers at the beginning of a piece of music are the **time signature**.

The time signature ²₄ tells us there are two of these crotchet beats
in each bar.

How many beats?

a semibreve or whole note   𝅝   equals 4 beats

a dotted minim or dotted half-note   𝅗𝅥·   equals 3 beats

a minim or half-note   𝅗𝅥   equals 2 beats

a crotchet or quarter-note   𝅘𝅥   equals 1 beat

a quaver or eighth-note   𝅘𝅥𝅮   equals ½ beat

a semiquaver or sixteenth-note   𝅘𝅥𝅯   equals ¼ beat

The names of notes

Each note represents a sound and has a letter name A B C D E F G.
This is where the notes are on the piano keyboard:

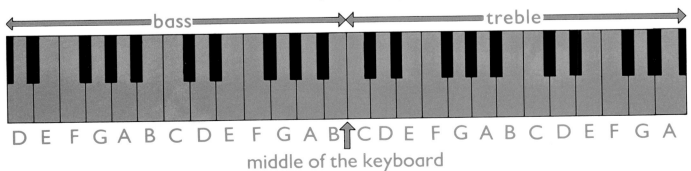

middle of the keyboard

Inside a recording studio

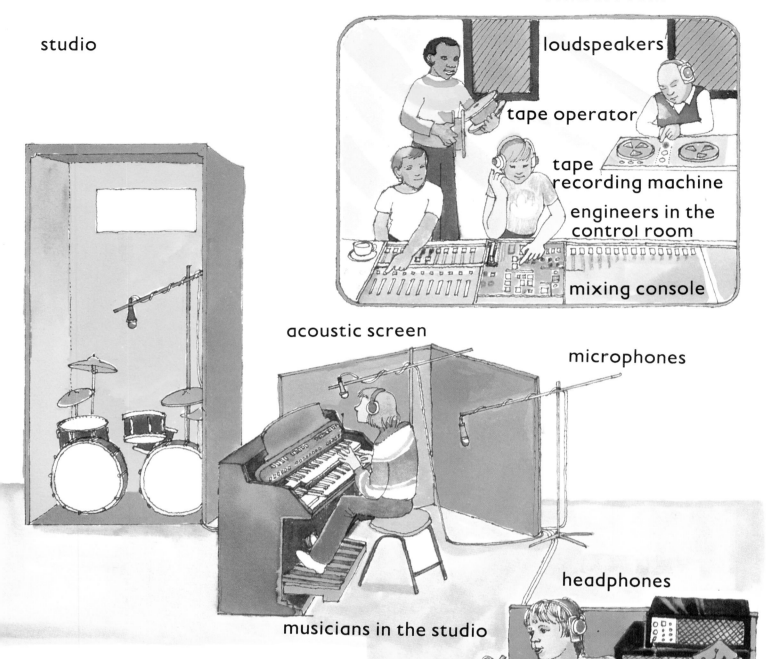

studio

control room

loudspeakers

tape operator

tape recording machine

engineers in the control room

mixing console

acoustic screen

microphones

musicians in the studio

headphones

Microphones in the studio send the sounds made by the musicians through the acoustic screen into the mixing console. In the control room the engineers adjust and balance the sounds before passing them through a tape recording machine. The tape operator edits the tape ready for final processing on to a record, tape or tape cassette.

Different types of music

Medieval

Folk

Western

Eastern

West Indian

Military

African

Natural

Synthetic and Computer

Music from around the world

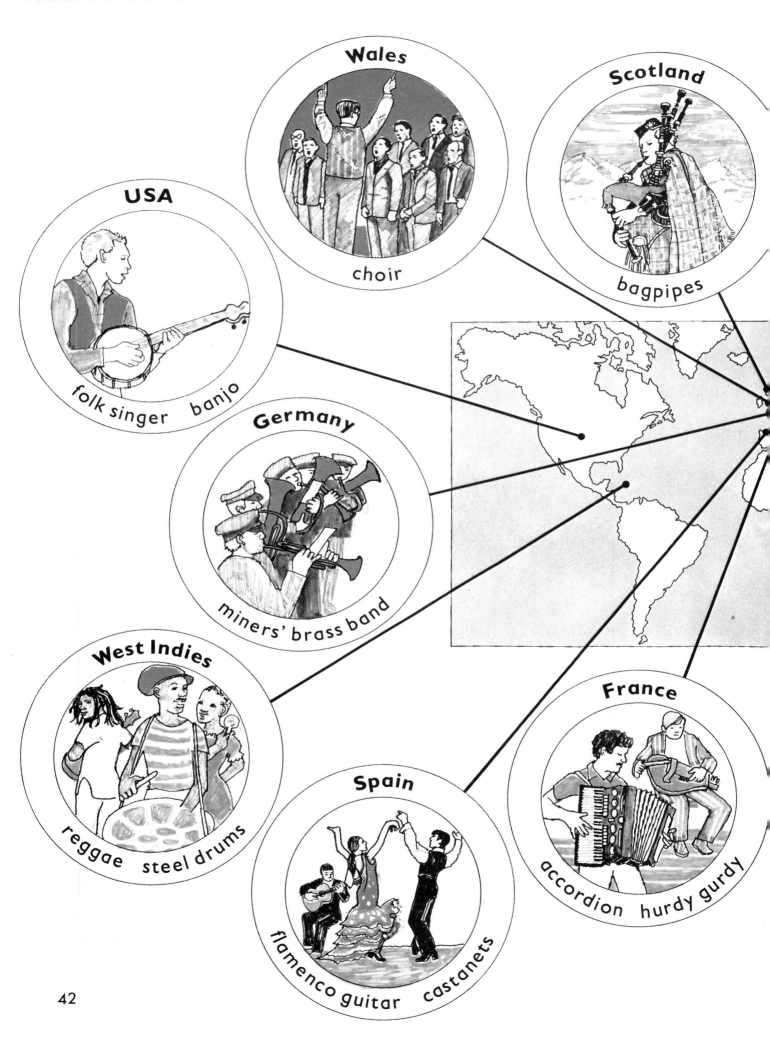

Wales — choir

Scotland — bagpipes

USA — folk singer   banjo

Germany — miners' brass band

West Indies — reggae   steel drums

Spain — flamenco guitar   castanets

France — accordion   hurdy gurdy

42

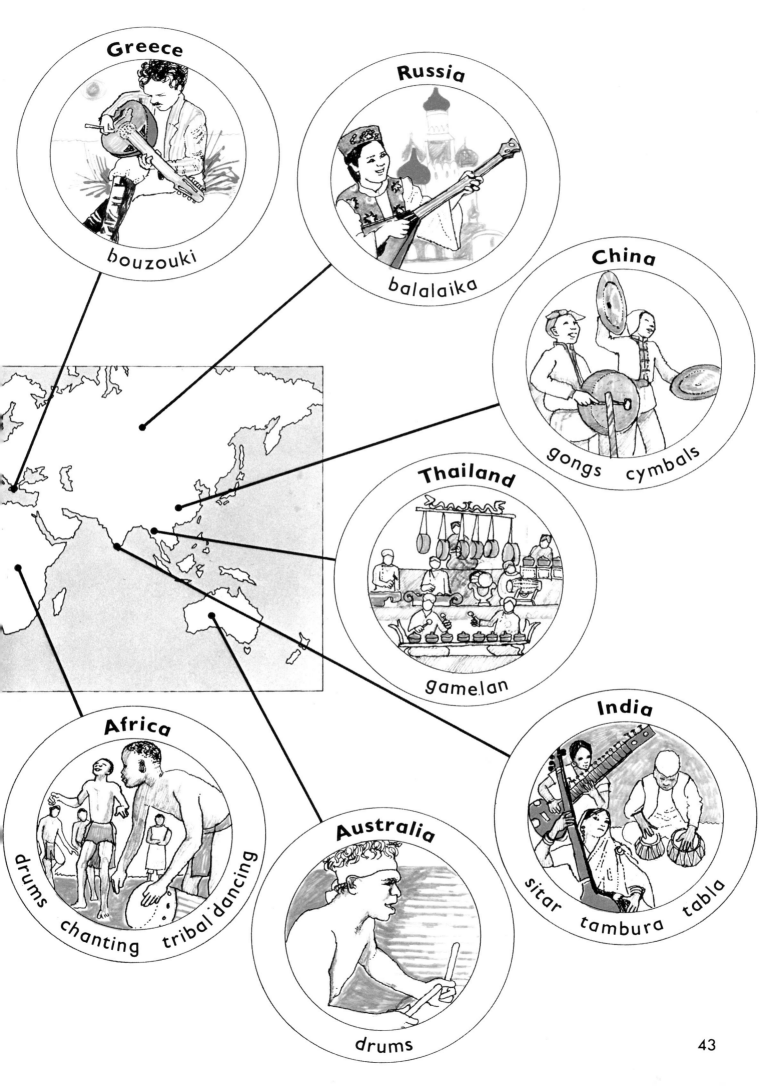

Greece
bouzouki

Russia
balalaika

China
gongs   cymbals

Thailand
gamelan

India
sitar   tambura   tabla

Africa
drums   chanting   tribal dancing

Australia
drums

43

Composers and the countries they come from

England
Austria
France
Norway

Italy
America
Germany
Poland

Czechoslovakia
Hungary
Russia

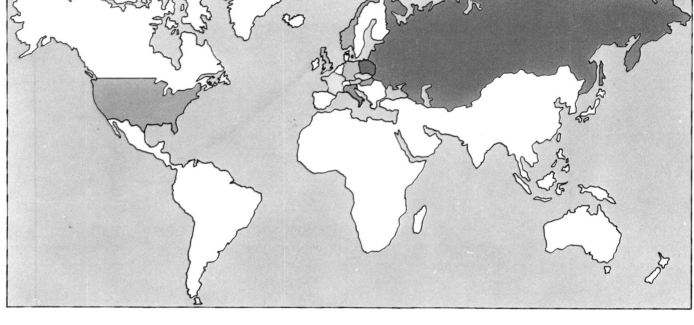

Edward Elgar
1857–1934
wrote the tune of
Land of Hope and Glory

Henry Purcell
1659–1695
wrote music for
fairy tale operas

Franz Schubert
1797–1828
wrote a lot of songs
including *The Erl King*

Benjamin Britten
1913–1976
wrote *The Young Person's Guide to the Orchestra*

The Beatles
a pop group in the
1960s and 1970s
wrote *Yesterday* and
Yellow Submarine

Joseph Haydn
1732–1809
wrote over 100
symphonies including
the 'Surprise'

William Gilbert
1836–1911 and
Arthur Sullivan
1842–1900
wrote a lot of
operettas

Peter Maxwell Davies
1934–
writes music for
children

Wolfgang Amadeus Mozart
1756–1791
started composing
when he was five

Maurice Ravel
1875–1937
wrote the ballet
Mother Goose

Claude Debussy
1862–1918
wrote piano music
for children

Edvard Grieg
1843–1907
wrote the *Peer Gynt*
suite

Gioacchino Rossini
1792–1868
wrote the opera
William Tell

Giacomo Puccini
1858–1924
wrote the opera
Madam Butterfly

Aaron Copland
1900–
wrote the ballet
Billy the Kid

Claudio Monteverdi
1567–1643
first great composer
of operas

Giuseppe Verdi
1813–1901
wrote a lot of
famous operas
including *Aida*

Scott Joplin
1868–1917
composer of the
ragtime piece *The Entertainer*

Johann Sebastian Bach 1685–1750
wrote a lot of
keyboard and
religious music

Karlheinz Stockhausen
1928–
uses electronic sounds
in his compositions

Robert Schumann
1810–1856
wrote piano music
for children

Ludwig van Beethoven
1770–1827 deaf from
an early age – wrote
'Pastoral' Symphony

George Frideric Handel
1685–1759
wrote music for a
firework display

Fryderyk Chopin
1810–1849
wrote a lot of piano
music

Antonín Dvořak
1841–1904
wrote the 'New
World' Symphony

Nikolay Rimsky-Korsakov
1844–1908
was influenced by
folk music

Sergey Prokofiev
1891–1953
wrote *Peter and the Wolf*

Béla Bartók
1881–1945
wrote Rumanian
carols for children

Peter Ilyich Tchaikovsky
1840–1893
wrote ballets
including *Swan Lake*

Igor Stravinsky
1882–1971
wrote the ballets
The Firebird and
Petrushka

Different songs

Lullaby   Hush-a-bye Baby

Hush - a - bye Ba - by   on   the   tree   top,

When   the   wind   blows   the   cra - dle   will   rock,

Calypso   Yellow Bird

Yel - low   bird,   up   high   in   ba - na - na   tree

Carol   Away in a Manger

A - way   in   a___   man-ger, no__ crib for a   bed,

Folk song   Kumbaya

Kum-ba - ya, my Lord, kum-ba-ya,   kum - ba - ya, my Lord, kum-ba - ya,

Nursery rhyme   Oranges and Lemons

Oran-ges and   le-mons, Say the bells of St.   Cle-ment's.

Hymn   Morning has Broken

Morn-ing has bro - ken   Like the first morn - ing,

Black-bird has spo - ken   Like the first bird._____

National anthem   God save the Queen

God save our gra - cious Queen,   long live our   no - ble Queen,

God save the   Queen.

Pop song   Yellow Submarine

In the town_____ where I was born Lived a man_____ who sailed to sea,

Opposites

high
low

soft
loud

big
little

light
heavy

fat
thin

whisper
shout

over
under

above
below

in
out

quick
slow

young
old

strong
weak

back   front

deep   shallow

sad   happy

up   down

stand   sit

play   rest

stop   start

before   after

inside   outside

eastern   western

DO YOU LIKE BUTTER?

question

YES.

answer

together   solo

Dances from around the world

USA

square dance

Ireland

jig

Caribbean islands

limbo dance

Spain

flamenco dance

Africa

dance to god of rain

Scotland

sword dance

Russia

cossack dance

Thailand

religious dance

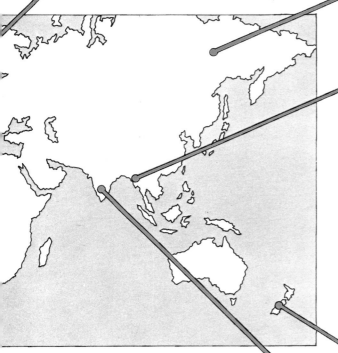

India

Radha-Krishna dance

New Zealand

Maori dance

Voices

Soprano
the highest voice

Alto

Tenor

Bass
the lowest voice

Different dances

Ballet dance
Swan Lake

Country dance
Maypole dance

Old-fashioned dance
a waltz

Folk dance
Morris dance

Modern dance
Disco dance

Stage dance
Tap dance

Festivals and musical occasions

Chinese New Year
a Chinese Festival

street decorations

flowers

lanterns

children's red
envelopes with
lucky money

sweets

fruit

fish
images

fire crackers

lion dancers

Lantern Festival
a Chinese Festival

fireworks

gong

cymbals

bells

lanterns

Passover
a Jewish festival

youngest
child

singing

chanting

lamb

watercress

nuts

apples

Seder

roasted egg

Haggadah

unleavened bread

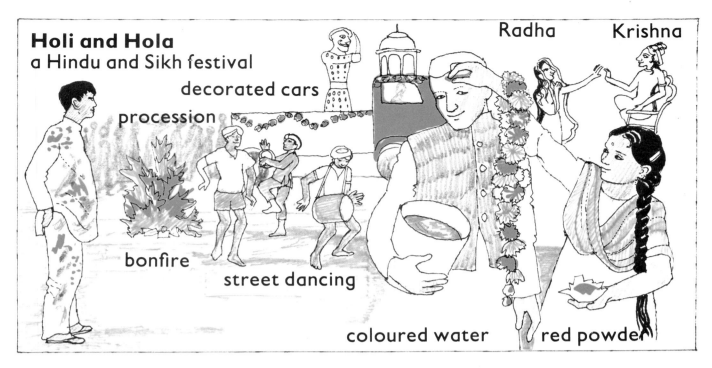

Holi and Hola
a Hindu and Sikh festival

decorated cars

procession

Radha   Krishna

bonfire

street dancing

coloured water   red powder

Carnival
a West Indian festival

limbo dancing

masks

maracas

dancing

fancy dress costume

steel band

lorry floats

Simchath Torah
a Jewish festival

synagogue

singing

dancing

procession

flowers

scrolls

Ganjitsu (New Year's Day)
a Japanese festival

decorations

children singing

playing instruments together

gifts   special meal

May Day
an English occasion

may blossom   maypole

procession   dancers

May Queen

pipe

fiddler   tabor   accordion

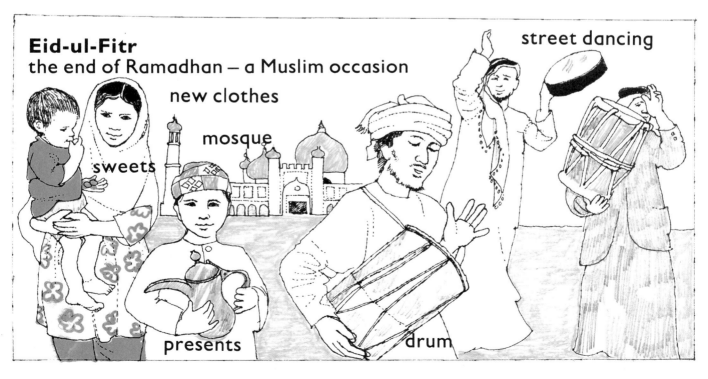

Eid-ul-Fitr
the end of Ramadhan – a Muslim occasion

street dancing

new clothes

mosque

sweets

presents   drum

55

Christmas
a Christian festival

star

carol singers

candles

decorations

Christmas tree

robin

nativity

presents

Obon
a Japanese Buddhist festival

circular folk dance

offerings to spirits

candles

Call to prayer
a Muslim occasion

minaret

mosque

dome

muezzin

prayer carpet

Qur'an

Dusshera
a Hindu Festival

procession

gifts

dancers

Sound and action words

loud words

bang
bash
belt
biff
bo!
boom

clang
clash
clatter
crash

din

roar

stamp
stomp

thump

whack

soft words

cuddle

hush

lullaby

moan

murmur

pat
pick
pluck

quiver

rock

shush!
slide
slither

tap
tickle
tiptoe

wander

ways of playing words

bang
blow

clash
clatter
click

flick

gaily

happily

jerkily

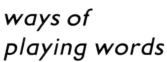

jingle

loudly

noisily

rattle
ring
roll
rustle

scrape
shake
smoothly
strum

tap
tinkle

ways of saying words

bark
boom

croak

falsetto

growl
grunt

hoot

loudly

moan
mumble
murmur

quickly
quietly

roar

shout
sing
slowly
softly
squeak
suddenly

unevenly

yell
yodel

ways of moving words

bounce
bump

crawl
creep

dance
dangle
dart
dither

flit
float

fly
frisk

halt
hop
hover

jerk
jollop
juggle
jump

kick
kneel

leap
lie
lightly

march

nod

over

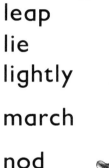

peep
pounce
prance

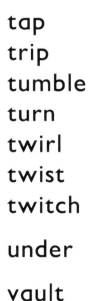

quake
quickly
quiver

reach
rumble
run
rush

shake
skip
slide
slip
spikily
stamp
steal
stealthily
stomp
stop
stumble
sway
swagger
swing

tap
trip
tumble
turn
twirl
twist
twitch

under

vault

waddle
walk
whip
whirl

Sound pictures

Some useful sounds to help you illustrate the pictures in this section

for scraping sounds

 sandpaper blocks

 rice, stones, small beads in a tube

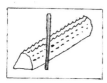 a guiro

 bamboo scraper

for watery sounds

 string of beads to drag across a glockenspiel or xylophone

 straw to blow through water in half-full milk bottle

 tube to blow through water in half-full bucket of water

 sandpaper blocks

for rattling sounds

 shakers, stones in a small pot

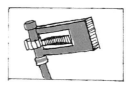 football rattle

 bottle tops

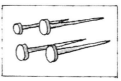 large nails

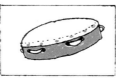 tambourine

 maracas

for buzzing sounds

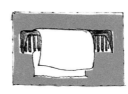 comb and tissue paper

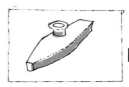 kazoo

for footsteps

 coconut shells

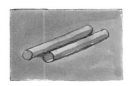 claves

 wood blocks

 xylophone

for popping sounds

 thick elastic bands stretched across a shoe box

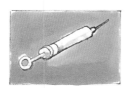 plastic syringe

 ping-pong balls in tin can

 stiff cardboard

for twinkling sounds

 Indian bells

 glockenspiel

 triangle

 large nails

for crackling sounds

 plastic egg boxes

 noisy cellophane

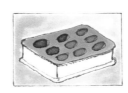 chocolate box moulding

Use your voice, hands, fingers, mouth, feet to help you too.

The four seasons

Find some things to help you make up the sound of

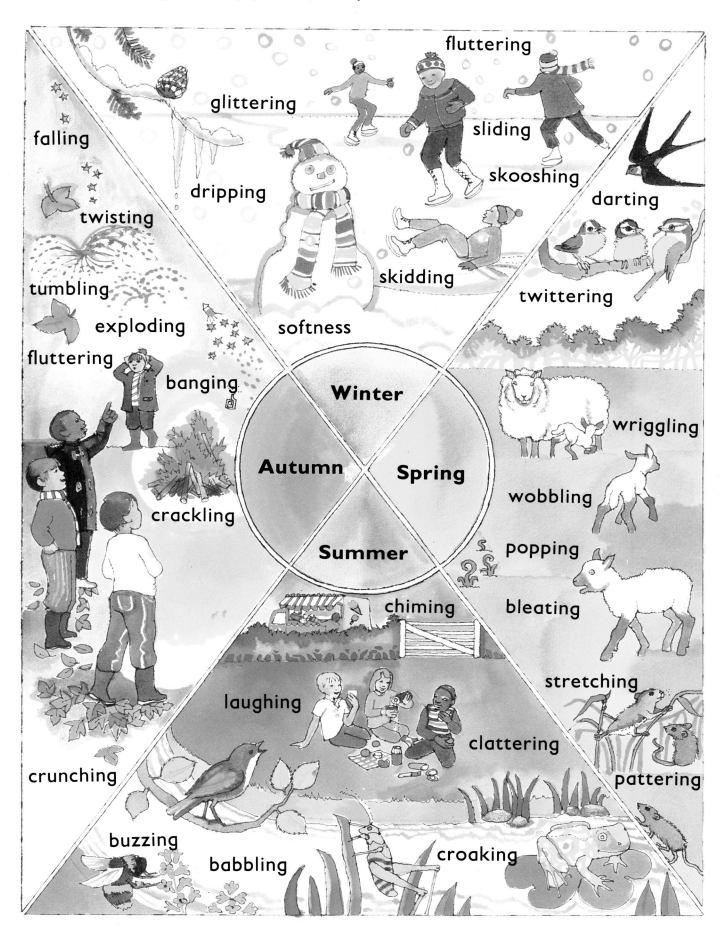

fluttering

glittering

falling

sliding

dripping

skooshing

twisting

darting

tumbling

skidding

twittering

exploding

softness

fluttering

banging

Winter

wriggling

crackling

Autumn

Spring

wobbling

popping

Summer

bleating

chiming

stretching

laughing

clattering

crunching

pattering

buzzing

babbling

croaking

A witch's cavern

Find some things to help you make up the sounds of

screeching

spitting

hissing

chuckling

splash

bubbling

fizz

plop

swishing

miaowing

purring

A walk in the rain

Find some things to help you make up the sounds of

sunshine

plopping

pattering

skooshing

tinkling

swishing

floating

splashing

walking quickly

shaking

Under water

Find some things to help you make up the sounds of

flapping

darting

flowing

bubbles rising

sparkling

echoes

shimmering

divers

snapping

banging

A farmyard

Find some things to help you make up the sounds of

brightness

chugging

crowing

stretching

clip-clop

hissing

splashing

pouncing

darting

scampering

pecking

63

The seaside

Find some things to help you
make up the sounds of

fluttering

building

patting

scraping

shivering

running

splashing

rippling

tooting

screeching

bumping

clip-clop

Journey into space

Find some things to help you
make up the sounds and shapes of

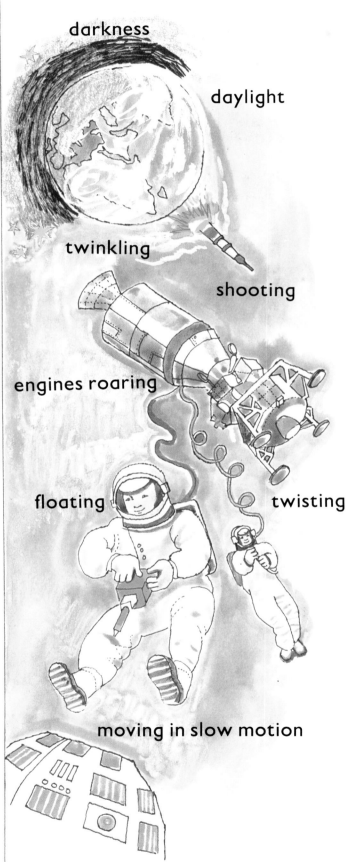

darkness

daylight

twinkling

shooting

engines roaring

floating

twisting

moving in slow motion